IOP Institute of Physics

Marvin and Milo

Adventures in Science

by Caitlin Watson

Illustrated by Vic Le Billon

45 experiments to do at home

Macmillan Children's Books

IOP Institute of Physics

The Institute of Physics is a scientific charity devoted to increasing the practice, understanding and application of physics. It has a worldwide membership of more than 36,000 and is a leading communicator of physics-related science to all audiences, from specialists through to government and the general public. Its publishing company, IOP Publishing, is a world leader in scientific publishing and the electronic dissemination of physics. www.iop.org

First published 2011 by Macmillan Children's Books
a division of Macmillan Publishers Limited
20 New Wharf Road, London N1 9RR
Basingstoke and Oxford
Associated companies throughout the world
www.panmacmillan.com

ISBN: 978-0-230-75849-0

Marvin and Milo cartoons (text and artwork) and illustrations
copyright © The Institute of Physics 2011
Additional text (on left-hand pages) copyright © Macmillan Children's Books 2011
Extra text written by Amanda Li

1 3 5 7 9 8 6 4 2

A CIP catalogue record for this book is available from
the British Library.

Printed and bound in China

Contents

Welcome to the world of Marvin and Milo!

Hi. I'm Marvin. And he's Milo. And we love doing experiments!

I usually come up with the ideas for all our challenges. But I couldn't do any of it without the help of my good pal Milo.

And Milo can't wait to see what new tricks I come up with — they're always a surprise!

They look just like an ordinary cat and dog but there's more to these furry friends than fluffy tails and wet noses. Most pets are only interested in where their next meal is coming from – but not Marvin and Milo! They want to know much more. They want to find out how the world works and why things float, fly and fall. And in their quest for knowledge these clever creatures perform loads of fun and fascinating experiments. The great thing is that you can do them all too – so follow Marvin and Milo's advice and 'Do try these at home'!

Bubbles are wonderful things. They're beautiful to look at, fun to make and fascinating to watch as they gently float through the air. Then – ping! – in an instant, they're gone!

Bubbles are made of trapped air, surrounded by a thin 'skin'. And, as you'll know, the best bubbles are made with soapy water. The soap reduces the surface tension, caused by the forces between the water molecules, and lets the skin 'stretch', letting you blow bigger, stronger bubbles. The bigger your blower, the more massive the bubble. It's even possible to make a bubble that will contain a whole person! (But you'll need a huge person-sized blower . . .)

Have you ever wondered why bubbles are always round? This is because a bubble is a special type of structure that tries to use the smallest possible surface area to hold the air contained inside it. And the shape that has the least surface area in relation to its volume is a sphere.

Now try Marvin and Milo's experiment and find out even more about bubbles!

Have you ever been 'shocked' when you put your hand on a door handle, or felt a 'crackle' when you walk across a carpet with your shoes on? This strange sensation is caused by static electricity. But where does it come from?

Any object that you can touch is made up of millions of atoms. Each atom is made up of particles called protons, electrons and neutrons. Protons carry positive charges while electrons carry negative charges. When certain materials come into contact with each other, electrons can be transferred from one to the other. The object that loses the electrons becomes more positively charged, while the object that gains them becomes more negatively charged. Opposite charges attract! So when a positively charged object comes close to a negatively charged object, the attraction between the two can cause electrons to jump across the space between them. The fast moving electrons heat the air and – bingo! – a tiny spark is produced.

Lightning is created in this way. Negative charge in the base of clouds builds up and starts to repel negative charges in the ground, leaving the ground with a positive charge. Eventually, the charges are so large that electrons leap from the cloud to the ground, heating the air and creating huge sparks – that's lightning!

BOTTLE BLASTER

Have you ever seen movies in which adventurers find themselves spinning around crazily, travelling through time and space? If so, you might have heard the word 'vortex' used to describe the scary, whirling mass that sucks them up. In real life, a vortex is usually a spinning body of air or water, such as a tornado or a whirlpool. You can even create a mini-vortex in a cup of tea by stirring it with a spoon! But there are other kinds of vortices around us which can't be seen with the naked eye.

Take bees, for example. The way in which they fly is a complicated business and one that scientists find quite hard to study (bees' wings being so small). Because of this, there are stories literally 'flying around' that bees can't fly! Now, this isn't true. The movement of bees' wings is really complex, but vortices play an important part in keeping bees happily buzzing around. Air swirls around in a vortex over the edge of the bee's wing, which helps 'suck' the bee upwards.

For more 'invisible' vortices take a look at Marvin and Milo's new idea. It's a blast!

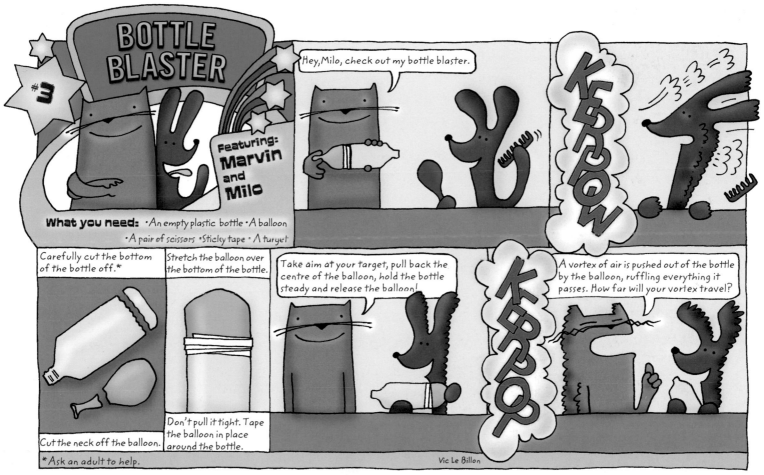

SPINNING JUICE

Marvin's latest experiment is all about gravity – the invisible force that affects every object in the universe. It keeps us on the ground and we feel the force of gravity as our weight. Gravity also keeps the planets in orbit around the Sun and causes the tides of our oceans. And you probably already know that it is gravity that makes objects on Earth fall downwards when you drop them.

Gravity pulls things towards the centre of the Earth, and it pulls all objects downwards at the same rate, whatever their mass. But if that's true, why, if you dropped a feather and a hammer from a tall building, would the hammer hit the ground first? The reason is air. The feather falls more slowly because the air surrounding it creates resistance and slows down its journey. If you were to drop a feather and a hammer in a vacuum (an environment where there is no air at all) they would both hit the ground at the same time!

Now try Marvin's water test and see what happens.

GLOWING ENVELOPE

In the seventeenth century Sir Francis Bacon wrote: 'It is well known that all sugar, whether candied or plain, if it be hard, will sparkle when broken or scraped in the dark.' But it wasn't just sugar that was seen to produce a spooky glow. A tribe of Indians called the Uncompahgre Ute used to fill buffalo hides with quartz crystals and shake them, fascinated by the strange glowing light that shone out. Since then we've discovered that this glow can also be seen when sticky tape and envelope glue is ripped apart in the dark.

Scientists still aren't completely sure how this glowing phenomenon – known as triboluminescence – occurs, but it seems that when certain substances are ripped, shattered or rubbed (crunching down on sugar crystals, for instance), areas of positive and negative charge are created. Jumping electrons collide with nitrogen molecules in the air and produce light. To most people this looks like a weird blueish-white glow. It can only be seen in the dark and it only lasts an instant – so keep your eyes peeled!

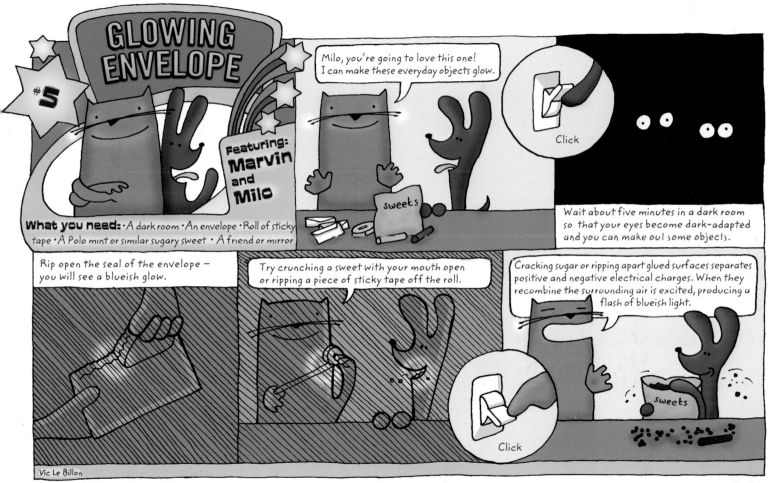

11

HEAD HANGER

Friction is a measure of how hard it is to slide one material over another. Whether you're rubbing your hands together for warmth, hitting a nail with a hammer or simply walking down the road, the force of friction is incredibly important. Without friction, life would be full of accidents! You'd slip over if there was no friction between your shoes and the ground, and the brakes on your bike or car simply wouldn't work.

The rougher two surfaces are, the greater the friction when they rub together. That's why trainers have deep treads on them to help grip the ground during sports. But smooth surfaces reduce friction and save energy. As you'll know, it's so much easier to cycle down a smooth path than down a rough gravel drive. But if it's too smooth (or even wet or icy) friction will be reduced and – whoops! – you will skid and slip.

Take a look at Marvin's latest trick to see what happens – or more accurately what *doesn't* happen – when friction is low.

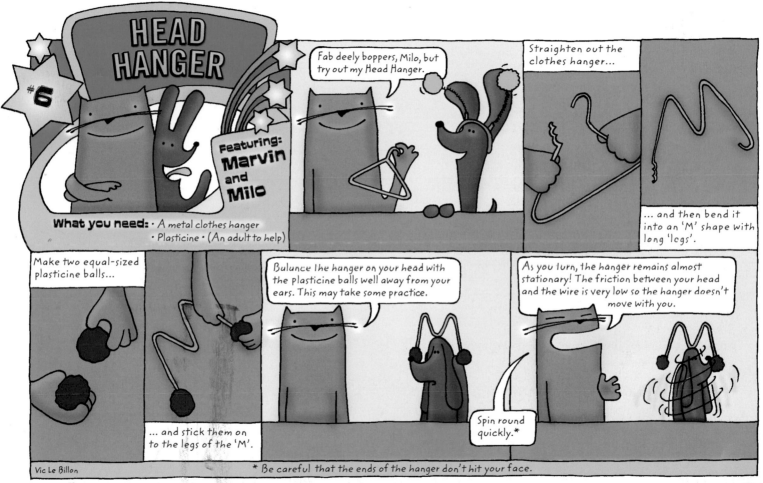

DRY DIVE

There are tiny particles of air – the atmosphere – all around us, pushing on everything, in all directions, all the time. This is known as atmospheric (or air) pressure but in everyday life we don't feel or notice it. And, luckily, we don't get squashed because our bodies are also full of air, which balances out the external pressure. But in outer space, astronauts can only survive if they wear special pressurized space suits that push against their bodies with the same force that they are used to on Earth.

You might notice the effects of air pressure if you've ever been to the top of a high mountain or flown in a plane. As you go higher, you'll experience a strange 'popping' sensation in your ears. This happens because the higher up we travel, the fewer air molecules there are in the atmosphere. The air pressure gets lower and your ears 'pop' to try to balance the different pressures between the inside and outside of your ears. It can be very annoying and sometimes a little painful.

Luckily, Marvin and Milo's watery trick is completely painless – and a lot of fun!

15

KEY DROP

Go for a spin with Marvin and Milo and you'll see gravity at work as well as something called 'angular velocity'. This describes how fast an object rotates and the direction it rotates in. Spinning balls, rotating planets and whirling ice skaters all have an angular velocity. One of the ways in which it is measured is the number of revolutions (turns) that occur per minute.

A spinning skater is lovely to watch even if the sight does make you feel a bit dizzy! When the skater starts off, he or she begins to spin slowly with their arms, and maybe a leg, spread outwards – the swing of their outstretched arms gives them the force they need to get moving. The rate of rotation, their angular velocity, depends on how their mass is spread out. To spin faster, they need to have their mass as close as possible to their body and so they pull their arms, and leg, in.

Voila – a superfast spin! When the skater extends their arms again, the spin slows down. Phew!

UPHILL BISCUIT TIN

As you know, on Earth, gravity pulls objects towards its centre so things drop downwards to the ground. They also roll downhill. Usually!

All objects have a centre of mass, and when this centre of mass is over the point where the object is in contact with the ground, the object is balanced. This is why you sometimes have to stick your arms out if you want to stand on one leg – you have to shift your mass in order to balance.

The centre of mass of an empty biscuit tin is in its centre. On a slope, the empty tin will feel the force of gravity through its centre of mass and it will roll downhill. But the centre of mass of a tin with some plasticine in it is no longer in the centre of the tin – it's close to where the plasticine is. Gravity still acts through the centre of mass and, on a gentle slope, the plasticine will be pulled downwards –

but this means that the tin as a whole will move uphill!

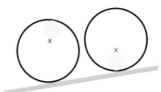

Although the centre of mass (marked with a cross) moves downwards, the tin rolls uphill.

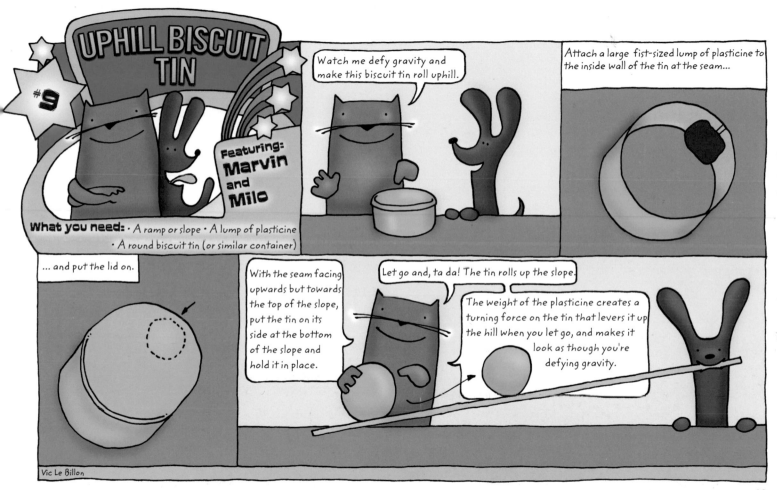

HOVERCRAFTY

Have you ever travelled on a hovercraft? You'd certainly remember if you had. A hovercraft is a vehicle that travels on a huge cushion of air. A fan blows air underneath the hovercraft platform and the air is trapped by a large piece of material called a skirt. The hovercraft gently rises up as it inflates before take-off.

Incredibly adaptable, air-cushion vehicles can travel on water, land and even on ice. Large hovercraft can carry many passengers and they are often used to make sea crossings. The trapped air must have enough pressure to support all their weight.

Another place where you might have seen a hovercraft-style motion in action is when you play air hockey. The disc that you hit – called the puck – floats on a thin cushion of air when the table is switched on. As there is hardly any friction between the puck and the table, the puck can move really fast!

Now go ahead and make your very own whizzy hovercraft!

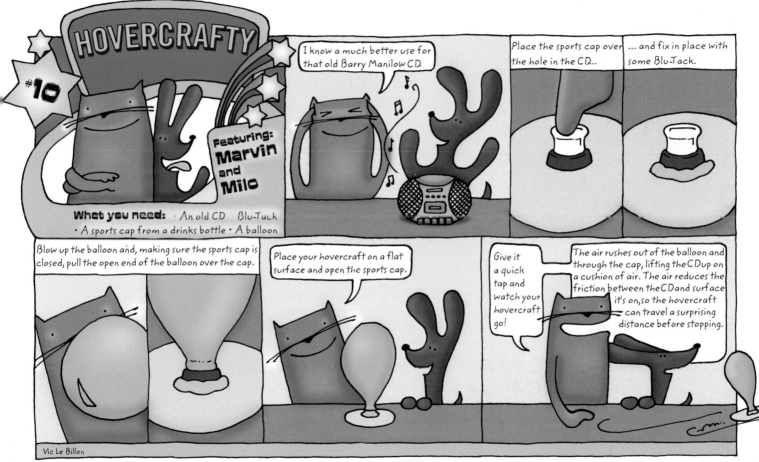

LOUD LOLLIES

Marvin and Milo are making music, though not with the usual kinds of musical instruments. They've discovered that sound can be made in lots of different ways – all it takes is for something to make molecules in the air vibrate. These vibrations are sound waves, which spread out in all directions, like ripples in a lake. Sound waves can travel through air and water and even solid materials such as wood and glass. Musical instruments usually have strings or reeds that create sound waves when they are plucked or blown.

You can feel sound vibrations if you wrap a piece of thin paper around a comb and hum or blow into it. You can also try putting your fingers on your throat. When you hum, you will feel the vibrations moving in your vocal cords. The faster the vibrations, the higher the pitch you hear. Now try Marvin's noisy lolly sticks!

Sir Isaac Newton was a great scientist in the seventeenth century who worked out many important ideas about physics, astronomy and mathematics. He developed three famous 'laws' which are called Newton's First, Second and Third Laws. These helped us to understand how things move and, to some extent, how the universe works.

In this experiment (though he doesn't realize it!) Milo is about to demonstrate Newton's Third Law, which says: 'For every action there is an equal and opposite reaction.' Newton realized that whenever two objects interact with each other, they exert forces upon each other. A person sitting in a chair exerts a downward force on the chair and the chair exerts an upward force on the person. These two forces are called action and reaction.

There are lots of examples of Newton's Third Law around us. When birds fly, for instance, their wings push the air in a downwards direction. But the air is also pushing the bird upwards. The force on the air is equal to the force on the bird. The same principle applies to a rocket, which lifts off by expelling hot gases from its engine. The rocket pushes on the gas and, in turn, the gas pushes on the rocket. Three, two, one – we have lift-off!

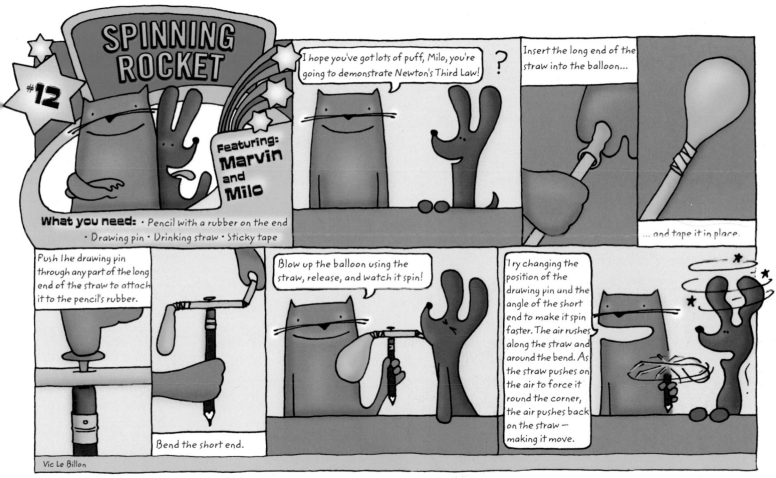

DAREDEVIL EGG

Dare you try Marvin's egg-citing experiment? Watch out for splashes!

The reason why the egg falls into the water takes us back to Sir Isaac Newton again, but this time the experiment shows Newton's First Law at work. This law is all about something called inertia. An object that is moving will keep on moving until a force acts on it to stop it. But if an object is still (our egg, for example) it will stay that way until a force acts on it and moves it. Both these objects are demonstrating inertia – the resistance to change in motion or rest.

In this experiment, when you hit the mat, the force of the blow moves the mat and the tube out of the way. But because of its inertia, the egg doesn't fly off to the side as well. The only force acting on the egg is gravity, and this pulls the egg downwards and into the water. Plop!

Marvin's completely loopy trick shows us how different forces acting on the cups make them weave around before diving down. Spin and lift can also be seen when a cricketer bowls a particularly tricky spin ball (known as 'curve ball' in American baseball) or when a tennis player hits the ball with a deadly spin that makes it curve fast through the air – and, of course, makes it extra-hard for their opponent to return.

Spinning balls, and cups, demonstrate an interesting principle called the Magnus Effect – named after Heinrich Magnus who wrote about it back in 1853 (though good old Newton had observed this effect many years before). Magnus described how air pressure was greater on one side of a spinning object while air was flowing past it. This greater pressure pushed the object to the side and made its path curve.

Without any spin, a ball is only affected by gravity pulling it downwards and air resistance slowing it down, so its trajectory – the path it follows – will be much more predictable and less curving. And much less exciting to watch in sport!

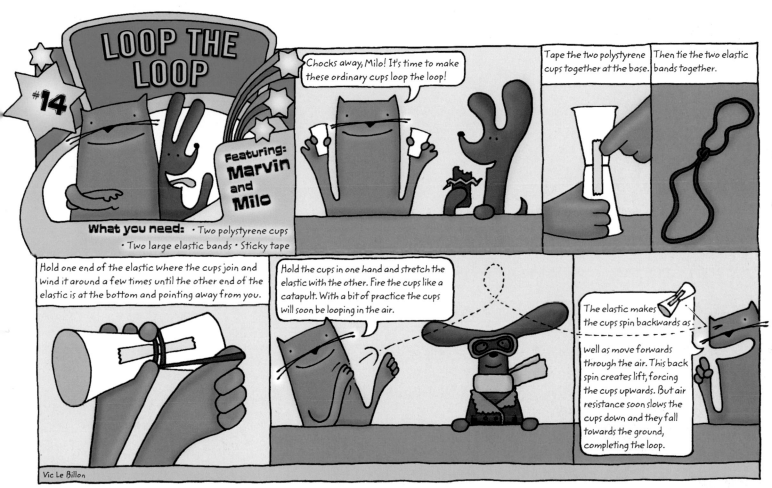

CLUMSY CATCHING

Whoops – butterfingers, Milo! This eye-catching experiment makes you realize how difficult life would be if you could only see with one eye. People who are impaired in this way find certain activities – such as catching a ball – much more difficult than someone with normal binocular (seeing with two eyes) vision. Actions like driving a car, threading a needle and pouring liquid from a jug will be very tricky for them. Watching a movie in 3D will be impossible.

So why is this? Humans have eyes positioned on the front of their heads, quite close to each other. Being about 65 mm apart, each eye perceives a slightly different view of things. You can compare views from each eye by closing each eye in turn, one after the other. The view is almost the same but the left eye sees more of the image to the left and the right eye

more of the image to the right. So how is it that we only 'see' one image in everyday life? Well, the two separate pictures are sent to the brain, which cleverly and instantly combines them to make one nice clear three-dimensional image. And which enables us to catch balls properly.

Now try the catching experiment and see how clumsy you can be!

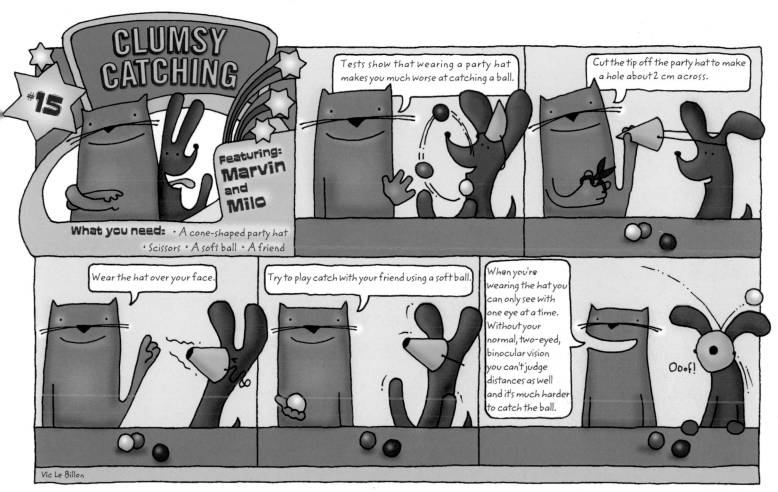

ON A ROLL

Roll up, roll up, for another great experiment with static electricity!

Have you ever rubbed a balloon on your jumper or hair and then stuck it to the wall? We knew you had! The balloon sticks, because it is attracted to the wall – and in Marvin's experiment the can is attracted to the balloon. Both are showing us the effects of static charge.

As you'll know from 'Quiche Lightning' all objects are made from atoms and all atoms contain particles called protons, which have a positive charge, and electrons, which have a negative charge. Atoms themselves are neutral because they usually contain an equal number of protons and electrons, which cancel each other out.

When certain materials are rubbed together, some of the electrons transfer from one to the other. One becomes more negatively charged and can be used to 'induce' an opposite charge in another object. The extra electrons on the balloon quickly repel the electrons in the wall and the can, making them both positively charged. As opposite charges attract, the balloon sticks to the wall and the can tries to follow the balloon!

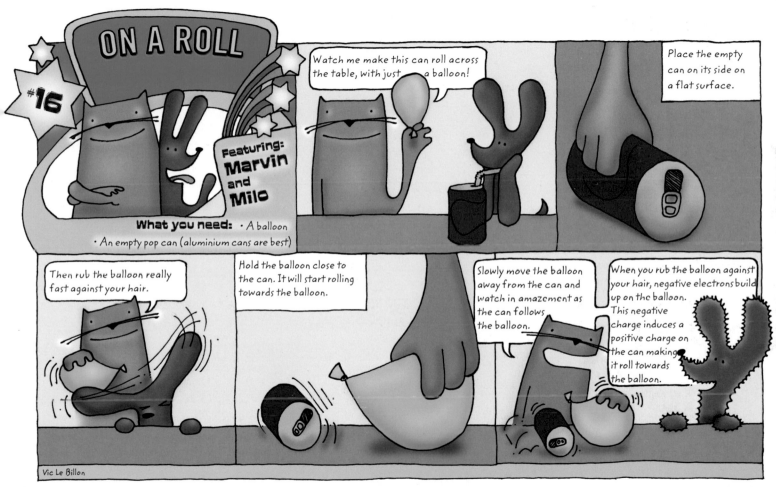

SECRET COLOUR

What Marvin's doing is called chromatography. This is a way of separating mixtures – in this case, ink. Black pen ink is a great substance to use because even though it *looks* black, it is actually made up of several different colours. Each of these colours is made up of molecules that are slightly different from each other when it comes to size and solubility. Solubility is how well they dissolve in different liquids – in this case, water.

The molecules travel at different rates when pulled along a piece of paper by the movement of the water – that's why the colours spread out over the paper. And as the water separates the different colour molecules, you can see the individual colours that make up the black ink. And, while doing so, create a colourful homemade 'rainbow'!

35

In this experiment the salt water keeps the egg in one piece, but why does the egg float in the salt water? It's because water with salt in it is denser than ordinary water. Density is a measure of how much mass something has in a given space. A dense object will be heavier than a less dense object of the same size. Compare a brick to a similar sized piece of foam rubber, and you'll certainly feel the difference!

An egg sinks in fresh water, but not in salt water, because the density of the salt water is greater than the density of the egg. Objects sink if their density is greater than the density of whatever they are trying to float in. But objects float if their density is less than the density of what they are floating in.

One of the most famous – and dense – bodies of water in the world is the Dead Sea. It contains a lot of salt – about 33 per cent by mass – and pretty much everything floats in it, even people who can't swim! In fact, the Dead Sea is so salty and dense that it's almost impossible to swim in it.

Now why not take up Marvin's suggestion and try dropping an egg without the salt water? You'll probably get a smashing result!

GRIPPING RICE

You'll really impress your friends when you tell them you can pick up thousands of grains of rice with a pencil! It just doesn't seem possible – but it is – and it's all down to our old friend, friction. When surfaces are rubbed together, friction is the force that resists the motion.

So what's happening when you 'stab' the pencil into the rice? The tip of the pencil pushes the rice outwards each time it is pushed into the jar. And each time you take the pencil out, rice settles into the space left by the pencil. As you do this again and again, the rice packs together more closely in the jar and the friction between each piece of rice and its nearest grains increases. After quite a few stabs, the friction between the pencil, rice and jar is so great that it is strong enough to hold up the jar by just holding the pencil. Gripping stuff!

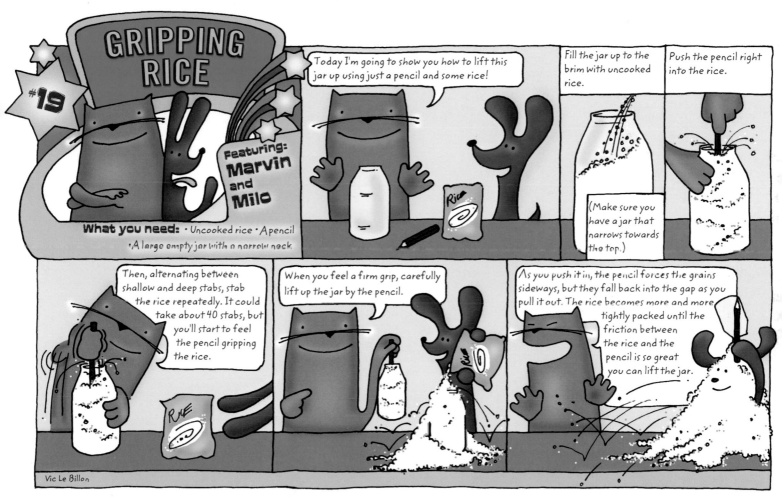

HOMEMADE SUNSET

Marvin's experiment not only explains why the sky appears red at sunset but also why the sky looks blue when it is sunny. It helps to know that white light from the sun is actually made up of lots of different colours. Red light has the longest wavelength and blue light the shortest.

The Earth's atmosphere contains air and water molecules. These absorb light from the sun and 'scatter' it in all directions. The blue light (because of its short wavelengths) is scattered more easily and we see a blue sky during the day because blue light is coming towards us from all directions. At sunset the sun is close to the horizon and the sunlight has to pass through more of the atmosphere to reach our eyes. This means that the blue light has been scattered away and we are left seeing the red light that we associate with sunset. Which is why the old saying goes: 'Red sky at night, shepherd's delight'!

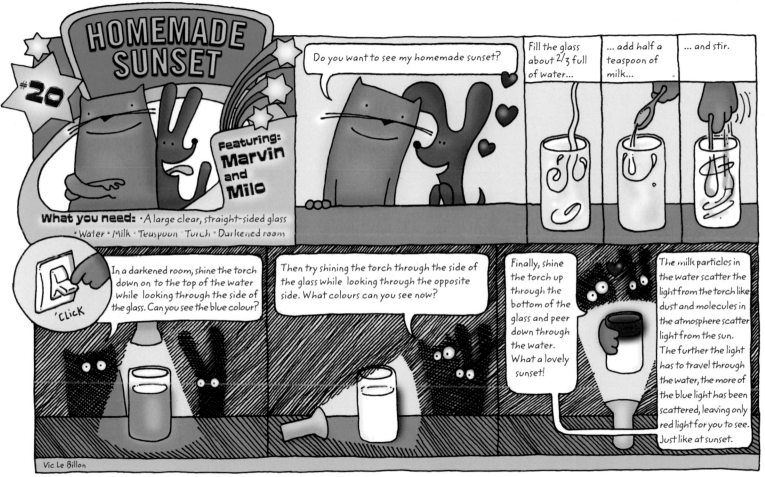

DANCING POP CAN

We all know what gravity is, more or less, but let's find out a bit more about this 'centre of mass' that helps the can dance in this experiment.

Well, every single thing (and that includes you!) has a centre of mass. If you take a ruler, you will find that you can balance it on one finger if you place your finger directly underneath its middle – that's the ruler's centre of mass. But not everything has a centre of mass in the middle. If you take a hammer – which is much heavier at one end – and try to balance it (you'll need one finger from each hand to do this), you'll find that you need to move your fingers much closer to the head – that's where the hammer's centre of mass is. Humans differ too – children have different centres of mass to adults.

It's all about balance. For any object to balance, the centre of mass needs to be directly above the balancing point. If it's not, the object will topple and probably fall.

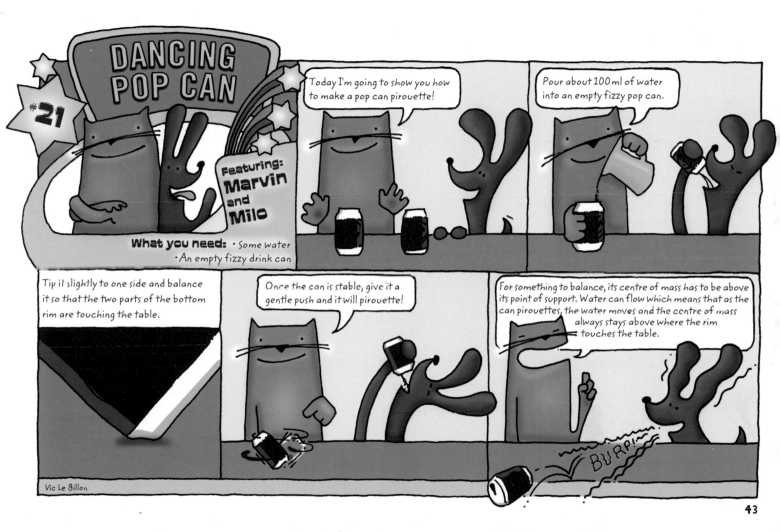

DANCING POP CAN

#21

Featuring: Marvin and Milo

What you need: · Some water · An empty fizzy drink can

Today I'm going to show you how to make a pop can pirouette!

Pour about 100 ml of water into an empty fizzy pop can.

Tip it slightly to one side and balance it so that the two parts of the bottom rim are touching the table.

Once the can is stable, give it a gentle push and it will pirouette!

For something to balance, its centre of mass has to be above its point of support. Water can flow which means that as the can pirouettes, the water moves and the centre of mass always stays above where the rim touches the table.

BURP!

Vic Le Billon

43

It looks as if Marvin and Milo have used a bucket of extra-strong glue for this experiment – but it's all down to the fantastic force of friction.

The pages of a book are made from paper, which may look nice and smooth, but under a microscope can actually be seen to have quite a rough surface. And we already know that the rougher a surface, the greater the friction.

Marvin discovered that when you interleave the pages of a book, the small amount of friction between each page adds up to a large force that is really tricky to overcome. Hence the very 'sticky' books!

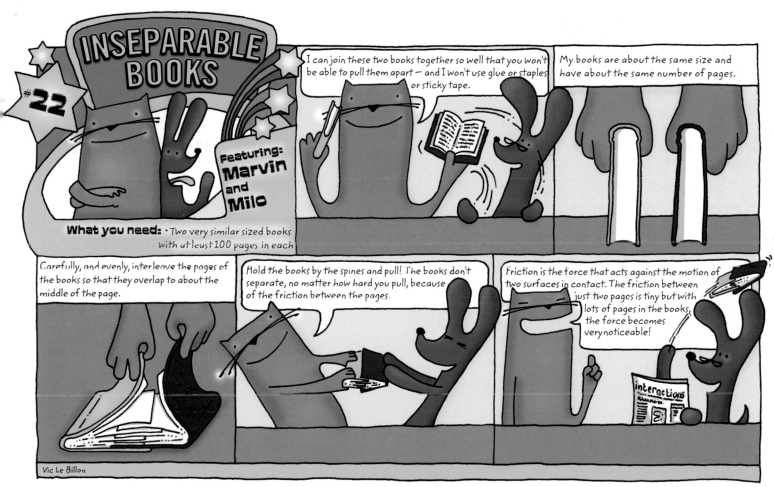

INSEPARABLE BOOKS

#22

Featuring: **Marvin** and **Milo**

What you need: · Two very similar sized books with at least 100 pages in each

I can join these two books together so well that you won't be able to pull them apart — and I won't use glue or staples or sticky tape.

My books are about the same size and have about the same number of pages.

Carefully, and evenly, interleave the pages of the books so that they overlap to about the middle of the page.

Hold the books by the spines and pull! The books don't separate, no matter how hard you pull, because of the friction between the pages.

Friction is the force that acts against the motion of two surfaces in contact. The friction between just two pages is tiny but with lots of pages in the books, the force becomes very noticeable!

interactions

Vic Le Billon

45

KETCHUP SACHET DIVER

Marvin's diving trick demonstrates a well-known scientific law called the Archimedes Principle. Archimedes was a Greek mathematician who is famous for shouting 'Eureka!' ('I have found it') at his moment of discovery. He had noticed that when he stepped into a deep bath the water overflowed – his body had pushed out or 'displaced' an amount of water proportional to the volume of his body. This breakthrough idea led to the Archimedes Principle, which states that any object put into a fluid is buoyed up by a force equal to the weight of the fluid displaced by the object.

When you squeeze the bottle in this experiment, the air bubbles in the sachet are compressed and the volume of the sachet reduces. This means it can displace less water, so the buoyant force acting on the sachet is smaller and it sinks.

When you stop squeezing the bottle, the air bubbles expand again, increasing the volume of the sachet and the amount of water that it can displace. The diver becomes what's known as 'positively buoyant' and up it comes!

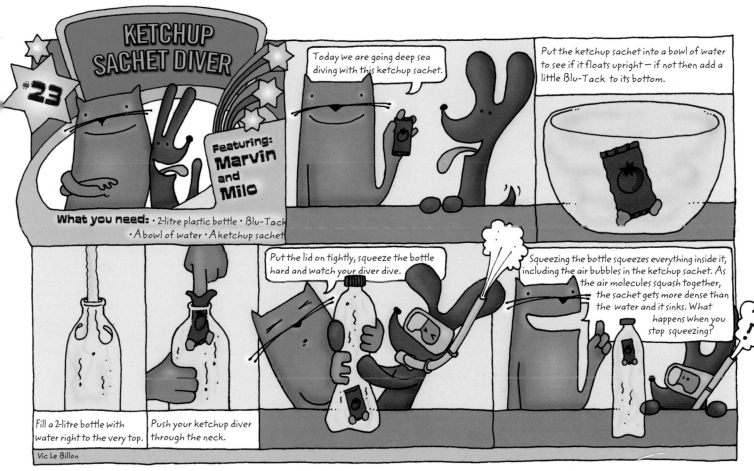

CHICKEN SOUNDS

Our ears are very sensitive organs. Even if you lightly brush your fingertips against your skin, you can hear a faint sound.

The intensity or 'loudness' of a sound is measured in decibels (dB). Humans can hear sounds over a huge range of intensities so the decibel scale is what's called 'logarithmic'. This means that while almost total silence is rated as 0 dB, a sound 10 times as loud is 10 dB, a sound 100 times as loud is 20 dB and a sound 1,000 times as loud is 30 dB. To give you an idea of what these numbers mean, a quiet whisper would be rated at around 15 decibels, a normal conversation would come in at around 60 decibels, while a gunshot or an exploding firework would be more like a massive 140 decibels!

In Marvin's experiment we hear the sound because the cup and the air inside it amplifies the size of the initial vibrations – the sound is made louder because the vibrations get bigger. A megaphone uses the same principle to allow people to be heard in crowds.

SINGING PAPERCLIP

As the wine glass demonstrates in this experiment, when an object vibrates, it causes movement in the air particles around it. These particles bump into other nearby air particles, making them vibrate and bump into even more air particles! These vibrations are sound waves.

The rate at which the air particles vibrate is called the frequency of the wave. The faster the air particles vibrate – that is, the higher the frequency – the higher the pitch of the sound you hear. Frequency is measured in hertz (Hz) after Heinrich Hertz, a German physicist.

As we get older, many of us lose the ability to hear higher-frequency sounds. But some animals have an amazing ability to hear the kinds of high-frequency sounds that no human could possibly detect. Bats, for example, not only hear high-frequency sounds, they also produce them! The sound waves that bats make bounce back from the surfaces of nearby objects and enable them to find their way around and locate prey.

INDESTRUCTIBLE BAG

As Milo soon discovers, when a pencil is taken out of the bag, water quickly comes bursting out! So if you don't want to end up wet like Milo, stand well back...

Try squeezing the bag tightly (over a sink or bowl, please!) and you'll see that the water comes out of the bag even faster. You might also notice that the water comes out more quickly at the bottom of the bag than at the top. This is because the speed of the water coming out of a hole depends on the amount of water above it. Water towards the bottom of the bag has a lot of water above it, so it is at a higher pressure than that towards the top of the bag.

You can feel this in a swimming pool – if you dive deep underwater you can feel the pressure of the water pushing on your ears. This pressure is much, much greater in the deep ocean. A submarine, or any other deep-sea device, needs a really strong hull to withstand the enormous pressure of the water. The deeper an object goes, the greater the pressure of the water on it. Heavy stuff...

It's fascinating to see how the water travels along Marvin's string in this experiment, rather than dripping downwards. This happens because of something called the Coanda Effect. In the 1930s an engineer called Henri Coanda noticed that a stream of air or fluid coming out from a nozzle tended to follow a nearby curved surface – even when the surface curved away from the original direction of the stream. So if a stream of water is flowing along a solid surface, which is curved slightly away from the stream, the water will usually follow the surface.

You can see this in action when flowing water 'sticks' to the underneath of a gently sloping rainwater gutter. The effect can also be seen with air. If you place a drinks can in front of a lit candle, then blow directly at the can, the air will 'bend' around the can and put out the candle. Clever!

The Coanda Effect is part of a science known as fluid dynamics, which is all about the motion of liquids and gases. It's something all aircraft designers know lots about!

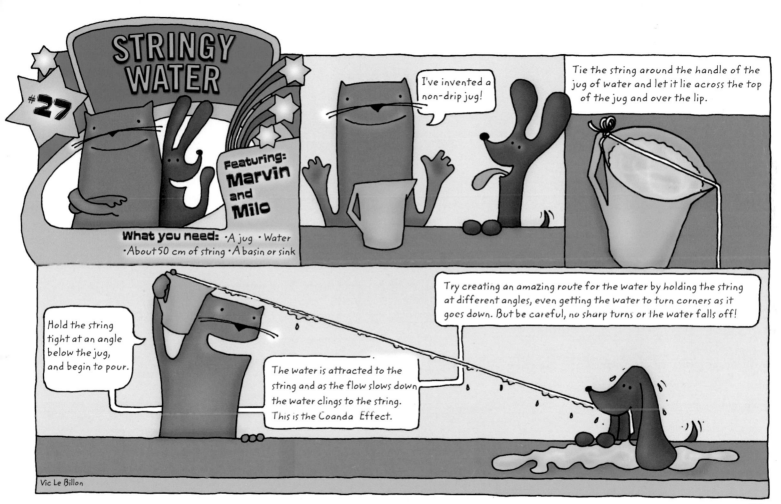

STRINGY WATER

#27

Featuring:
Marvin
and
Milo

What you need: · A jug · Water
· About 50 cm of string · A basin or sink

I've invented a non-drip jug!

Tie the string around the handle of the jug of water and let it lie across the top of the jug and over the lip.

Hold the string tight at an angle below the jug, and begin to pour.

The water is attracted to the string and as the flow slows down the water clings to the string. This is the Coanda Effect.

Try creating an amazing route for the water by holding the string at different angles, even getting the water to turn corners as it goes down. But be careful, no sharp turns or the water falls off!

Vic Le Billon

Marvin's experiment certainly proves that atmospheric pressure is all around us. As you're reading this book, atmospheric pressure is pushing on every part of your body from your fingers to your toes, but you don't even notice it!

Atmospheric, or air pressure, is the force exerted on an area by the weight of tiny and invisible particles (molecules) of air above that area. The column of air above your head and shoulders, stretching up to the top of the atmosphere, weighs about a tonne and exerts a pressure of one atmosphere on you – this is normal air pressure.

Atmospheric pressure can be measured by an instrument called a barometer. When there's high pressure in a region, the air molecules are more densely packed together so there's a greater mass of air pushing on you. With low pressure, there are fewer air molecules so there's a lower pressure. Measuring and predicting differences in air pressure is really important for weather forecasters.

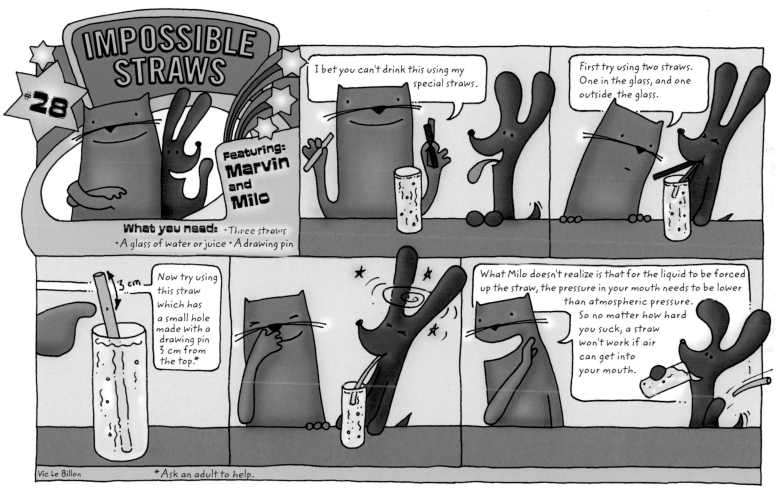

SIMPLE SIPHON

Marvin's magical 'drinking' bowl shows us a cunning way of moving liquids – via a siphon. Siphons like this can even be used to move water uphill! Try Marvin's technique, but use a longer straw or piece of tubing and try to get the water over a pile of books. As long as the second bowl remains lower than the first, the water will flow.

This siphon works because the 'downhill' part of the tube is longer than the 'uphill' part and so has more water in it. The force of gravity on this greater mass pulls the water down the tube and the water in the 'uphill' part follows.

You might not think that you've ever used a siphon before, but some flush toilets contain a 'bowl siphon'. The characteristic 'sucking' sound of a flushed loo is the sound of the siphon emptying out the toilet bowl!

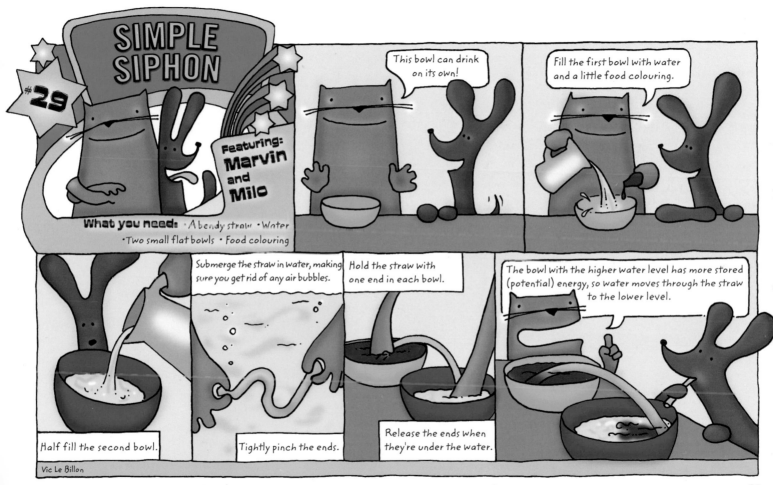

The result of this experiment is curious. If you touch the frying pan it feels slightly colder than the plastic bowl – so why does the ice cube melt faster on the pan?

How fast the ice cube melts depends on how fast heat can be transferred to it from its surroundings. When heat is transferred from one object to another it is called conduction. A material such as metal is a good conductor because it allows heat to move through it quite easily and quickly. Because the ice cube is colder than the frying pan, heat is conducted from all over the pan into the cube – so the cube melts more quickly.

So why did the pan feel cold when you first touched it? As it is a good conductor, when you put your warm finger on the frying pan, heat was quickly conducted away from your finger. This makes the pan feel cold.

The plastic bowl, however, is not a good conductor of heat – in fact, it's an insulator. It feels warmer when you touch it because it doesn't transfer the heat from your finger very well.

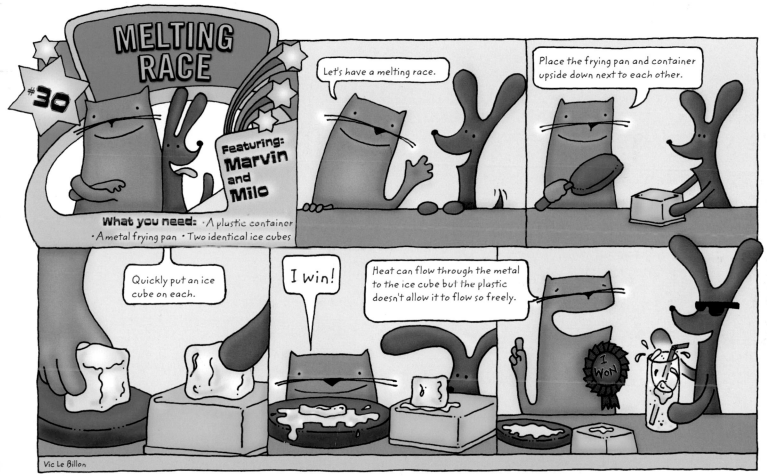

In 'Spinning Rocket' on pages 24–25 we saw Marvin demonstrate Newton's Third Law – which says that for every action there is an equal and opposite reaction. So when an object exerts a force on another object, the second object also exerts a force on the first object.

As you already know, this principle is very important for jet engines and space rockets, which need this force – called jet propulsion – in order to move. But did you know that jet propulsion is also used by some living creatures? If you've ever seen an octopus or a squid moving along in the water you'll know how. Like your balloon rocket, an octopus propels itself by forcing a substance through an opening at high speed. In this case, seawater! The octopus squeezes water out of its funnel-shaped opening (a bit like the opening of the balloon) and the force of the escaping jets of water make it move in the opposite direction. Newton's Third Law in action under the sea!

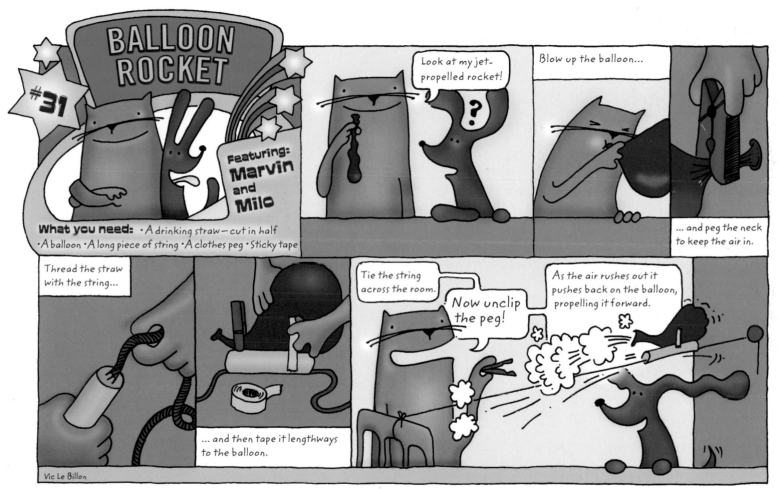

63

REVERSING GLASS

Marvin has noticed that the glass of water acts like a lens – but what is a lens exactly?

The word 'lens' actually comes from the Latin meaning 'lentil', because of its shape. You might know that a lens is a part of the human eye, but it is also what we call a piece of curved glass or plastic that focuses rays of light and forms an image. Lenses like these can be found in magnifying glasses, microscopes, spectacles, telescopes, cameras and many other objects.

Marvin's water bends the path of the light and reverses the image you see. Another way of seeing that water bends, or refracts, light is to put a straw into your glass. If you look at the side of the glass, your straw looks bent or broken at the point where it breaks through the water. This is because when light travels from one substance to another, for example from air to water, its speed changes and this causes a change in direction. Thus producing a broken straw. Truly mindbending!

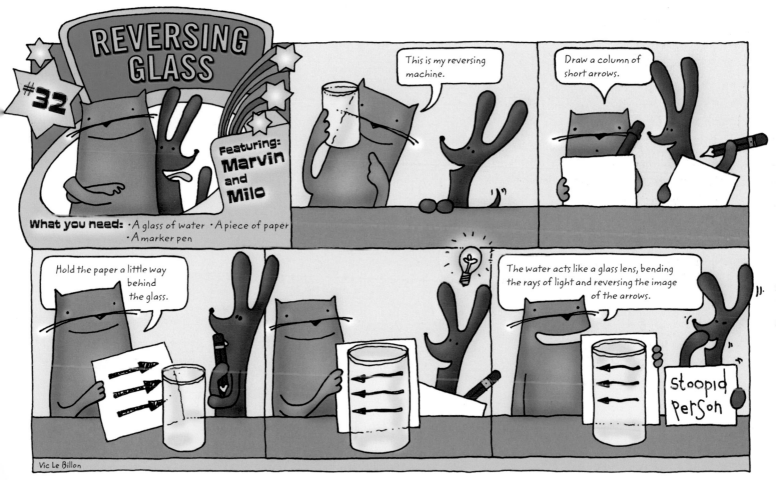

Marvin's bouncing balls show how momentum is conserved. The momentum of something is worked out by multiplying its mass by its velocity – how fast it's going in a certain direction. The bigger or faster an object is, the more momentum it has.

If you look closely when you do this trick, the lower, bigger ball hits the ground first and, as it bounces back up, it knocks into the smaller ball, which is still falling. During the collision, some of the larger ball's momentum is transferred to the smaller ball, which then goes flying off. The smaller ball may bounce higher than before, but if you're still looking closely, you'll notice that the bigger ball bounces less – so the overall amount of momentum remains the same as when the two balls are dropped separately. Now that's what we call fair play!

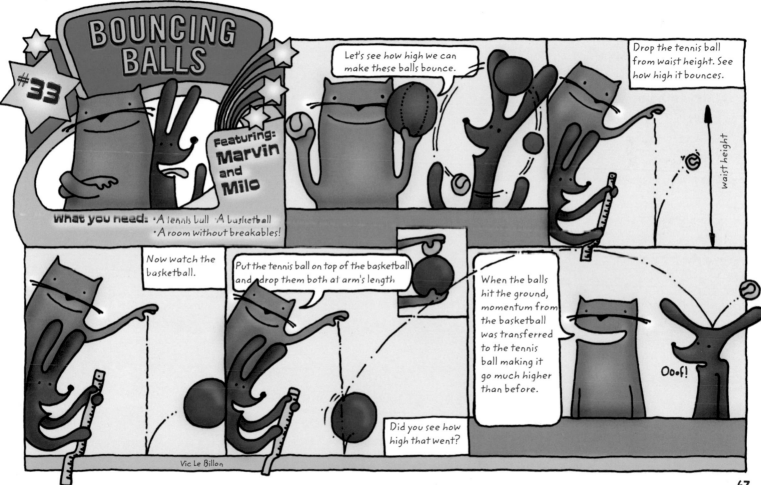

CONVECTION SNAKE

Marvin's moving snake shows us that, though we can't see them, the particles in the air around us are also moving.

When anything heats up, its molecules start to move about faster. The hotter something is, the faster its molecules are moving. All this rushing about means that things expand – take up more space – when they heat up. This is easiest to see in gases as the molecules are already well spaced out and moving about. When a gas, such as air, heats up and expands, it becomes less dense – there are fewer molecules in a given space. You may already know that hot air rises and this is because the warmer, less dense air can float on top of colder, more dense air.

This movement of air because of differences in temperature, and therefore density, is called convection. Radiators heat rooms by convection –

they heat the air close to them, which then expands and moves away to be replaced by cooler air that is then heated, expands and moves away.

But it's not just things around the home that make use of convection. Powerful convection currents in the air help create clouds, winds and rain. Even earthquakes and volcanoes are caused by massive convection currents in the molten magma (hot liquid rock) under the Earth's crust.

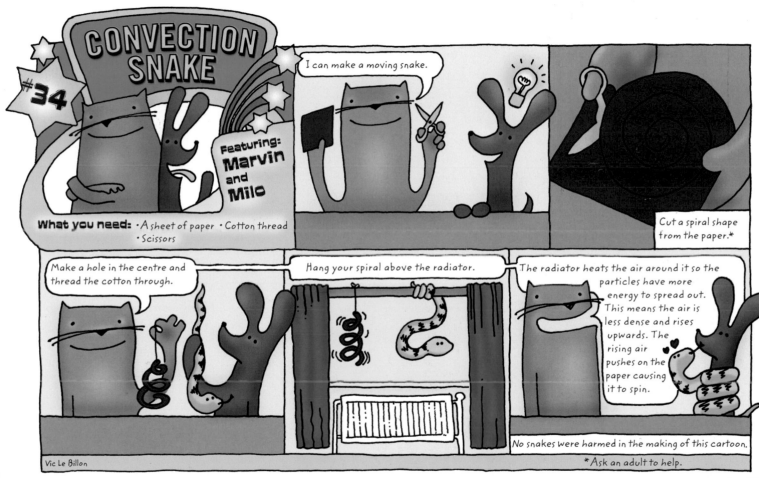

FOIL BOAT

Impressed by Marvin's moving boat? It may look like magic – but it's all about molecules.

Water molecules are what are called polar molecules – one end of a water molecule has a positive charge and the other end has a negative charge. This means that water molecules are attracted to each other. At a water surface, the molecules are strongly attracted to the molecules below and this 'surface tension' forms a kind of skin.

To see the effects of surface tension, turn a tap on a tiny bit, so that a drip slowly forms. Watch the drop get bigger and bigger. Surface tension is what holds the drop together, clinging to the tap, until the drop gets so big that its weight overcomes the attraction between the water molecules and it finally falls!

Some insects, such as pond skaters, can walk on water without sinking because of the water's surface tension – you can see the tiny dents that their feet make in the water.

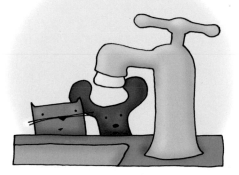

71

WOBBLY STICK

Marvin's wobbling stick rotates around its centre of mass – the point at which an object can be balanced. With a perfect sphere, the centre of mass is right in the middle. We know this because, if the sphere was supported at the centre, it would be perfectly balanced and would spin evenly. But finding the centre of mass of an object isn't always so easy, especially if the object has an odd shape or its mass isn't evenly spread out.

Clever old Archimedes first thought about the idea of a centre of mass, using levers, weights and floating objects to demonstrate his theories. He also worked out a mathematical technique for finding the centre of mass for a triangle – it's actually close to its base.

Racing cars are designed to have their centre of mass close to the ground, rather than in the centre of the car. This allows the racing car to make impressive high-speed turns. And if Marvin makes any more high-speed turns on that stick, it'll be Milo that starts feeling wobbly!

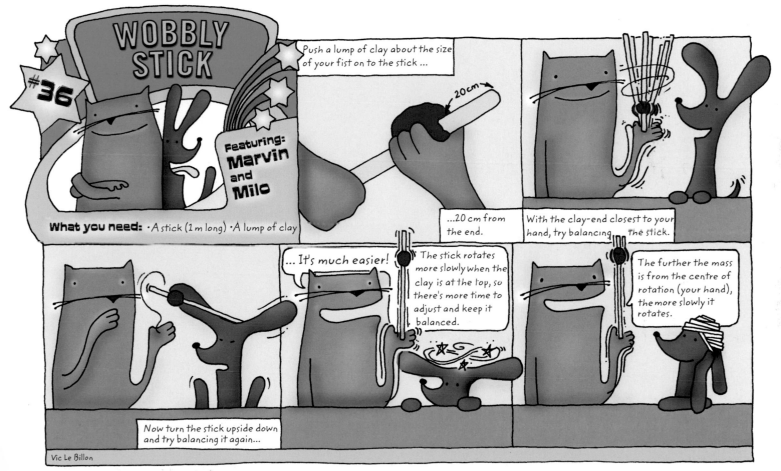

73

MAGIC TOOTHPICKS

As Marvin and Milo know, wood is a very versatile material, one that has been used by humans for hundreds of thousands of years for building houses and making furniture, ships, musical instruments, sculptures and all kinds of other things.

Wood can be sawn and bent and cut into many shapes and sizes. But it is important for all woodworkers to know that wood can expand (get bigger) and contract (get smaller) depending on how much water it contains. This is because wood is a porous material – nature has designed it so that when it was a living tree it could draw up water from the ground. If you looked at a piece of wood under a microscope, you would see that it is made up of long fibres, a bit like bundles of straws, which once helped it to 'suck' up water.

So, depending on the season, wood might absorb moisture from its surroundings, and expand. But when the air is dry, the same wood will dry out and slowly contract, becoming smaller. You might have noticed that wooden doors are more difficult to open at certain times of the year – this is because the wood has expanded and made the door 'stick'.

You might think that sound would travel much more easily through air than through something solid – but as Marvin and Milo prove, this isn't the case!

When you tap the coat hanger in this experiment, the vibrations travel all the way through the metal, along the string and through your finger bones, ending up at your ears. Inside your ear the sound waves reach your eardrum, a thin piece of skin stretched tight like a drum, causing it to vibrate. The vibrating eardrum moves three tiny bones inside your ear. These are called the hammer, the anvil and the stirrup, because of their unusual shapes. The bones move the sound waves along on their journey into the inner ear, where they are heard by you as sound.

If you try this experiment without your fingers pressed against your ears, you'll find that all you can hear is a faint tapping sound. This shows that the metal guides the sound waves to your ears rather than them spreading out in all directions through the air.

MAGIC BALLOON

Air pressure isn't something we are normally aware of, but – as in Marvin's experiment – differences in air pressure can make us sit up and take notice. You might have felt a tingling sensation in your ears, or even felt them 'pop', when taking off or landing in an aeroplane. This is caused by the sudden change in air pressure as the plane changes height.

You may also have seen weather forecasters talking about air pressure on TV. This is because it has a big effect on the type of weather we get. Windy days, for example, are the result of air moving quickly between regions of different air pressure.

But unlike temperature, moisture and wind, you can't easily work out what the air pressure is through your senses. Only a weather forecaster, or an instrument called a barometer, can tell us about this.

SEW AN ICE CUBE

We know that salt melts ice. It's why salt is scattered on icy roads when freezing weather hits. But how does this happen?

Adding salt to water lowers its freezing point – a lower temperature is needed for the salt/water mixture to freeze than pure water. Even at zero degrees C, the freezing point of pure water, solid ice will still have some liquid water molecules on its surface. If the temperature falls, these liquid molecules will eventually join the regular structure of the ice and freeze. However, adding salt messes up this regular structure and prevents the water molecules from joining the solid.

At the same time, normal melting continues to take place – at zero degrees C, some solid ice molecules have too much energy to remain as part of the solid and become liquid. Adding this to the action of the salt preventing liquid water molecules from becoming solid ice explains why the ice melts.

Marvin's trick only uses a small amount of salt, so while the top layer of the ice cube melts, it quickly refreezes and buries the thread in ice. You might even find that you can dangle Marvin's ice cube from the thread. Cool!

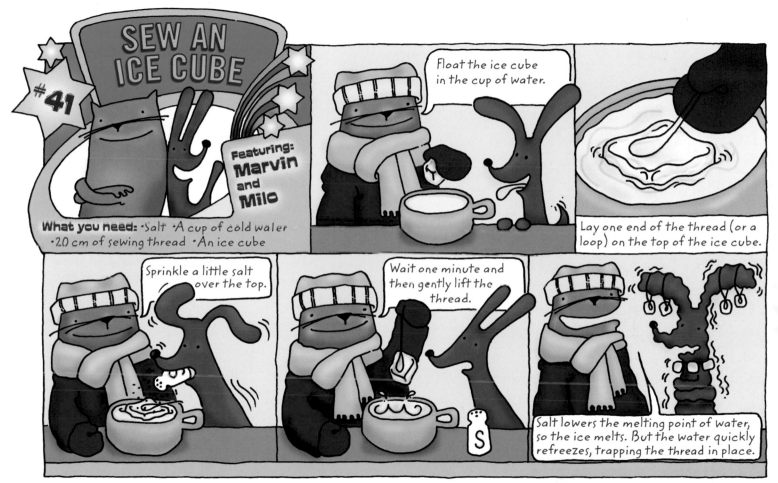

SPINNING EGGS

This is a really clever way to tell a raw egg from a cooked egg without breaking the eggs!

The reason why the raw egg keeps spinning is down to our old friend Newton and his First Law of Motion, which states: 'An object in motion remains in motion, unless acted upon by an external force.' In other words, if something is moving, it'll keep moving unless something else stops it. When you put your finger on the shell, the friction between your finger and the shell makes it stop, but the liquid inside continues to spin for a while longer, causing the shell to spin again when you remove your finger.

You might also notice that your raw egg wobbles and spins more slowly than the cooked egg. When you spin the raw egg, the position of its centre of mass changes as the fluid inside the egg sloshes about – hence the wobble. Your solid egg has an unchanging centre of mass and should spin nice and evenly.

Egg-citing stuff, Marvin and Milo!

Marvin's great experiment lets you 'bend' water – and it's all down to static electricity. As you saw in 'Quiche Lightning' (pages 4–5) and 'On a Roll' (pages 32–33), objects around us can become electrostatically charged. When you put a dry comb through your hair, some of the electrons on the hair are transferred to the comb, making it negatively charged. The negatively charged comb 'induces' a positive charge in the water – it repels the electrons in the water so that the water closest to the comb becomes positively charged and bends towards the negative comb. You can do this experiment with other things too – instead of water, try salt sprinkled on a table or small bits of torn-up paper. Other objects that can be used instead of a comb are a balloon or a ruler.

Another fun thing to try when you're doing this experiment is to wiggle the comb around close to the stream of water. If your comb has enough charge, the attraction could be strong enough for you to direct the stream of water as you wiggle the comb!

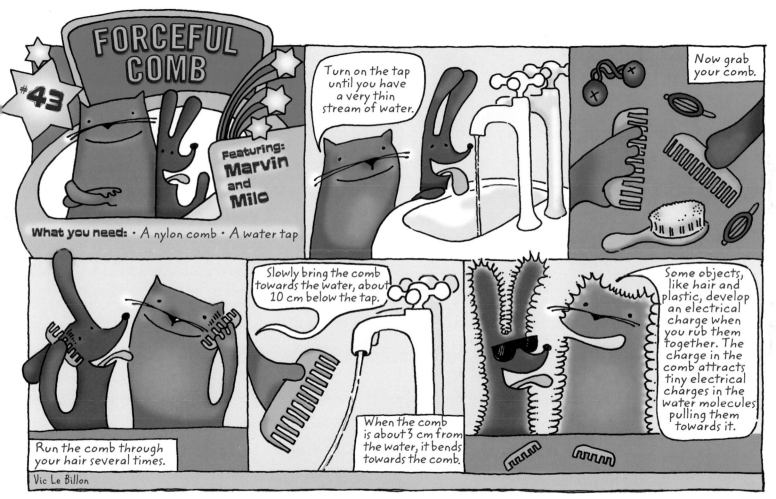

STRAW WATER GUN

Splash! Another surprising result from Marvin and Milo.

Marvin's straw trick shows us that fluids move from areas of higher pressure to areas of lower pressure. This is exactly what happens when you use a normal straw to drink a glass of water. When you suck through a straw, you remove air from inside the straw and the atmospheric pressure on the outside of the straw is now greater than the pressure inside the straw. So as the atmospheric pressure pushes down on the surface of the water in the glass, water is forced up through the straw and into your mouth.

There are also other forces at play when it comes to straws. One is called capillary action. Capillary action describes how liquids climb the walls of a tube and it is what helps the water 'cling' to the insides of your straw. It is very important for plants.

Something called viscosity – the 'runniness' of a liquid – also affects your drinking ability. If a liquid is highly viscous, you will have to suck much harder. A thick milkshake is a great example – much harder to suck through a straw than water. But probably tastier!

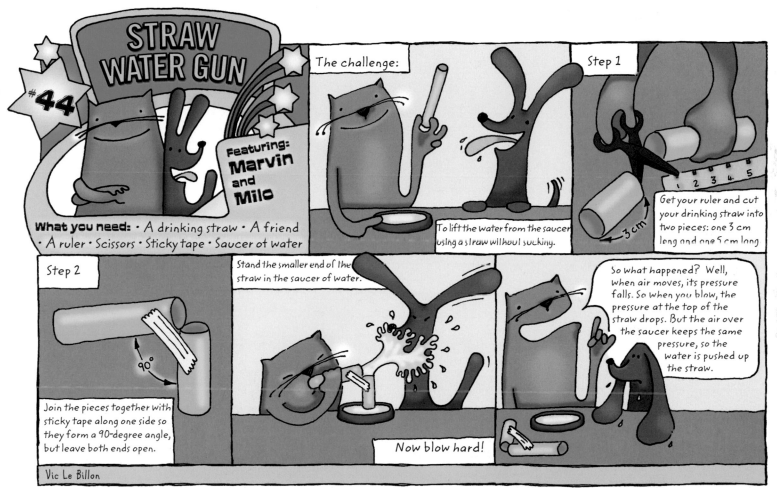

MAGIC APPLES

Once you've done Marvin's amazing apple experiment, why not try a similar test with two empty fizzy drink cans? Place them on their sides, with just a small gap in between. If you blow between the two cans, what do you think will happen? You've guessed it, the cans will actually move closer together! Just like the apples, your blowing has increased the air speed between the cans and lowered the air pressure. The higher air pressure on the outside surfaces of the cans pushes them together.

This principle is extremely important in shipping, as it applies to liquids as well as gases. Ship's captains and crew know that two ships passing each other can be in danger of a sideways collision. Why? Because water flowing between the two ships is forced into travelling more quickly than water flowing past the outsides. The water pressure goes down and the pressure on the outer side of the ships forces them together. So the two ships must be steered slightly away from each other to avoid an accident!

About the Author

Caitlin Watson is Physics in Society Manager for the Institute of Physics. She has been writing experiments for Marvin and Milo to try out since 2005. Other Institute employees, including Elizabeth Jeavans and Nicola Hannam, have also contributed to the monthly adventures of Marvin and Milo. The intrepid cat-and-dog team originally appeared in *Interactions*, a newsletter for members of the Institute of Physics, and can also be seen at www.physics.org and www.facebook.com/pages/Marvin-Milo/30754874738

About the Illustrator

Victoria Le Billon lives in Bristol and divides her time between working as a graphic designer, an illustrator and a mum. Marvin and Milo were conceived back in 2004 for the Institute of Physics *Interactions* newsletter and during that time have had their antics translated across the globe, appearing on behalf of the Institute of Physics in South America, South Africa and even Wales.

For more information on Victoria Le Billon visit: www.billybonbon.com